The Aristocats is based on the book by Thomas Rowe.
Published by Hachette Partworks Ltd.
ISBN: 978-1-908648-67-9
Date of Printing: June 2013
Printed in Malaysia by Tien Wah Press

THE ARISTOCATS

Looking for
the Aristocats

Disney

Hachette

At the Aristocats' home, it was a day like any other. The kittens, Marie, Toulouse and Berlioz, played together while their parents looked on lovingly.

Duchess was very proud of her kittens. They were such cute little bundles of fun! Their father, O'Malley, was just as proud. Before he met Duchess, O'Malley had lived on the streets, but now he was a respectable family cat.

That afternoon, O'Malley took a stroll round the garden and met one of his friends, a big, grey cat.

"I've just heard that our friend Cyril is ill," said the cat. "Shall we go and visit him?"

"Of course," replied O'Malley. "Poor Cyril must be bored. Let's go and cheer him up!"

As he followed his friend out of the garden, he called out to Duchess, "I'm going out for a while. I'll be back for dinner!"

"See you later!" called Duchess as O'Malley sauntered through the gate and out onto the street.

At teatime, Duchess and the kittens had warm
milk in the kitchen. Mmm! It was delicious.

"Hello there, friends!" squeaked a voice
from a hole in the corner of the kitchen.
It was Roquefort the mouse.

Roquefort's favourite treat was a biscuit dunked in milk, and the kittens were happy to share their teatime snack with him.

After tea, it was time to play. Toulouse let Roquefort use his tail as a swing.
"Higher! Higher!" laughed the mouse.

After the game, Duchess told the kittens that
it was homework time. Roquefort scampered
back to his hole while Berlioz played piano and
Marie practised her singing.

Toulouse began painting a beautiful bouquet of flowers.

After a while, Duchess decided to go for a nap. "Carry on with your homework, and don't get up to any mischief," she told the kittens.

Poor Duchess. If only she knew what was in store!

No sooner had Duchess left the room than the naughty kittens began to do exactly what they had been told not to do – get up to mischief!

The kittens chased each other along the piano keys, then Toulouse used his picture as a trampoline, covering the canvas with paint paw prints!

Just then, Marie
noticed that the
window had been left
open. This opportunity
was definitely too good
to miss! The kittens
clambered out into
the garden.

"Shall we go to the end of the street?"
suggested Toulouse.
"Good idea!" agreed Marie.
"Let's go!" said Berlioz.

Meanwhile, Duchess had woken from her nap and couldn't believe her eyes. The house was in a total mess – and where were the kittens?

She looked under the bed…

… and in the clothes trunk.

Perhaps they were finishing their bowls of milk?

She raced down to the kitchen, hoping she would find the kittens there.

But the kittens were nowhere to be found. Duchess was very worried.

Duchess jumped up to the window and peered out, but she couldn't see the kittens in the garden.

"What's the matter, Duchess?" asked Roquefort. "You look worried. Can I help?"

"The kittens have disappeared, and O'Malley isn't here!" cried Duchess.

"O'Malley is so smart, he knows every street in the city," she continued. "I'm sure he'd find them in no time. But I don't know my way around at all – I'd be sure to get lost! Will you help, Roquefort?"

"Of course I will," replied the little mouse. "I'll find O'Malley and we'll have those kittens home in no time!"

Roquefort hurried back to his hole and put on his detective's cape and hat. A good investigator must always look the part!

As soon as he was dressed, Roquefort scurried off to begin his search.

"Now, where can O'Malley be?" the mouse wondered. "I know! I'll bet he's with his friends."

Be careful, brave Roquefort! The city is a dangerous place for a little mouse...

... and the greatest of all dangers to a little mouse is a cat! Suddenly, a huge, sharp-fanged cat appeared from behind a dustbin.

"Hey, where are you going?" snarled the cat.

A terrified Roquefort turned and ran for his life.

As the cat caught up with him, Roquefort ran inside an old drainpipe.

Luckily for Roquefort, the cat was too fat to follow him inside. The little mouse raced to the other end of the pipe and escaped. Phew, that was a close shave!

As soon as he got his breath back, Roquefort continued his search. "Where can O'Malley be?" he muttered to himself.

Suddenly, he found himself face to face with three mean-looking cats. Taking a deep breath, Roquefort asked them, "Excuse me, gentlemen, can you help me?"

The cats sniggered. A mouse asking a cat for help? They couldn't believe it!

The biggest cat seized Roquefort by the tail. "So, my little friend, how can we help?" he leered.

"I'm l-l-looking… for O'Malley," stammered the mouse. "Duchess needs him. It's an emergency!"

Immediately, the cats stopped teasing Roquefort. This was serious!

The cats led Roquefort to Cyril's house. O'Malley
was amazed to see the little mouse.

"C-come quickly," gasped Roquefort. He was
so out of breath he could hardly speak. "Duchess
needs your help!"

"What's happened?"
asked O'Malley.
"The kittens have
gone!" replied Roquefort.

"You'd better go and find
them," said Cyril to O'Malley.
"And thanks for coming
to see me!"

"Follow me, Roquefort," said O'Malley. "We'll search on the rooftops first."

"B-but isn't that a bit dangerous?" said Roquefort nervously.

"The kittens are always trying to imitate me," explained O'Malley. "So they might be up here. If not, I'll bet those little rascals have gone fishing!"

O'Malley was right. At that very moment, the kittens were on the riverbank.

"Let's use this basket as a boat," suggested Toulouse.

"All aboard!" cried Berlioz. The kittens clambered into the basket and floated out onto the river.

But the current soon carried the basket far away from the bank. The kittens began to feel scared.

"HELP!" shrieked Marie and Berlioz.
"If only O'Malley was here," whimpered Toulouse.

Just then, Roquefort and O'Malley, who were perched on the railing of a nearby bridge, heard frantic meowing from below.

"Look, it's the kittens!" shouted Roquefort,
pointing at the little basket bobbing in the water.
"We have to rescue them!" cried O'Malley.

"But how?" squeaked Roquefort. "I can't swim! Can you?"

"Yes, I can," declared O'Malley. "Jump on my back and hold on tight. Ready… here we GO!"

SPLASH!

O'Malley, with Roquefort clinging onto him for dear life, dived into the icy water.

O'Malley began to swim, but it was hard
work keeping afloat in the strong current.

"Basket ahoy!" cried Roquefort suddenly. Sure
enough, a few metres away, O'Malley spotted
the three kittens.

O'Malley swam as hard as he could towards the basket. The bedraggled kittens were huddled together, scared stiff and feeling very seasick!

"Hang on, I'm here!" yelled O'Malley.

"O'Malley! Roquefort! Thank goodness you're here!" cried the kittens. They looked relieved, but also ashamed of disobeying their mother and getting themselves in so much trouble.

One by one, O'Malley dropped the kittens onto dry land. They were a very sorry sight!

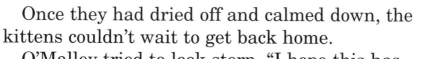

Once they had dried off and calmed down, the kittens couldn't wait to get back home.

O'Malley tried to look stern. "I hope this has taught you all a lesson," he said. But he was so relieved that they were safe he couldn't help smiling at his naughty kittens!

When they got home, Duchess was waiting at
the window. Her face was like thunder! The kittens
knew they were in for a big telling-off.

"You must all be punished," began Duchess angrily.

"My dear," interrupted O'Malley. "Perhaps they have been punished enough. They got such a fright that I don't think they'll do anything like that again!"

"Yes, we promise we'll be good from now on," pleaded the kittens.

Duchess' face softened a little. "Well, I hope you have learned your lesson," she said. "Now, shall we all go and have a warm bowl of milk?"

"YES, PLEASE!" cried the kittens as they raced towards the kitchen. They had already forgotten all about their scary adventure.

Marie, Berlioz and Toulouse crouched at their bowls and lapped up their milk hungrily.

Suddenly, they heard a squeak. "Hey, don't forget me!" said Roquefort. "Leave me some milk so I can dunk my biscuit!"

When they had finished their meal, the
exhausted kittens snuggled up in their basket.
Soon, they were fast asleep.

"They're so cute when they are asleep," smiled
O'Malley. "Too bad it never lasts long!"

"My dear O'Malley, you were so brave!" said
Duchess admiringly.

"Me? I didn't do much," said O'Malley modestly.
"The real hero is Roquefort – the best mouse
detective in all of Paris!"